Ferrer
School

A Piece of Straw

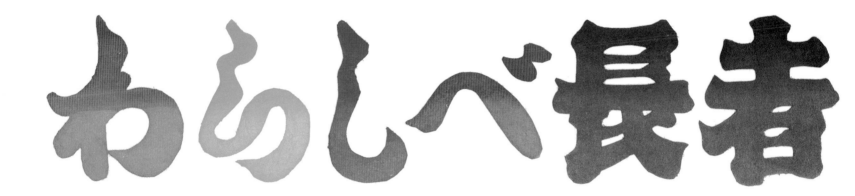
わらしべ長者

For Bill Senior and Teruko

© Illustrations JUNKO MORIMOTO 1985
© Adaptation HELEN SMITH 1985
First published 1985 by William Collins Pty Ltd, Sydney
First Published in Paperback 1986
Typeset by Savage Type Pty Ltd, Brisbane
Printed in Japan by Dai Nippon Printing Co Ltd
Designed by Anna Warren

National Library of Australia
Cataloguing-in-publication data

A Piece of Straw.

For children.
ISBN 0 00 662331 X
1. Tales – Japan. I. Morimoto, Junko.
398.2'0952

A PIECE OF STRAW

illustrated by
Junko Morimoto

FONTANA PICTURE LIONS
Collins Australia

There was once a man whose name was Yohei.
He had a kind heart but,
alas, he was very poor.
Every day he would go to the shrine
and ask for help
to find a good job.

On the day of Yohei's hundredth visit
to the shrine, the air suddenly turned cold
and in the chill wind came a message.
"Take heed of that
which first comes to your hand."

Yohei ran from the shrine,
"Hooray! Hooray!" he called,
then CRASH!
He landed at the foot of the stone step,
and there he lay.
Suddenly Yohei realised
that he was holding something in his hand.

It was just a piece of straw.
Yohei was disappointed,
but not discouraged.
To brighten the straw up
he tied a passing horsefly to the end,
and off he went.

"Waa...Waa...Waa..."
The peace of the day was shattered.
A small boy was screaming and crying.
His poor mother looked very worried,
she just didn't know how to calm him.

"What's the matter?
How can I help?" asked Yohei.
"Here, look at this,
would you like it?"

Yohei amused the little boy
with his horsefly straw.
Soon the crying stopped
and the little boy brightened up,
his sorrows forgotten.

"Oh, thank you, thank you,"
repeated the mother,
"Please, take these mandarines
they are very sweet."

So Yohei exchanged his horsefly straw
for the sweet mandarines
and with a hop and a skip
on he went.

Not long after, Yohei came upon a traveller
slumped by the roadside,
his face was deathly pale and he was moaning.
"What's the matter? How can I help?" inquired Yohei.
"Ooh, I have travelled too far, too fast,"
groaned the traveller,

"I am so thirsty I think I am going to die."
"Don't do that," said Yohei, "I have just the thing for you.
Here, eat these sweet mandarines
and you will feel much better."
With a small sigh of regret, Yohei watched as his mandarines
were thirstily eaten by the traveller.

The traveller soon felt much better
and was on his feet again.
He turned to Yohei,
"You are a generous man.
Please accept these
as a token of my gratitude."

Yohei was dumbfounded.
In his hands he now held
two beautiful rolls of silk.
Never had he dreamed of owning such treasure.
And so, his heart singing with joy, on he went.

Yohei carried the rolls of silk
with great care.
Ahead of him on the road
was a tremendous commotion.
A horse lay collapsed in the dirt,
unable to move.

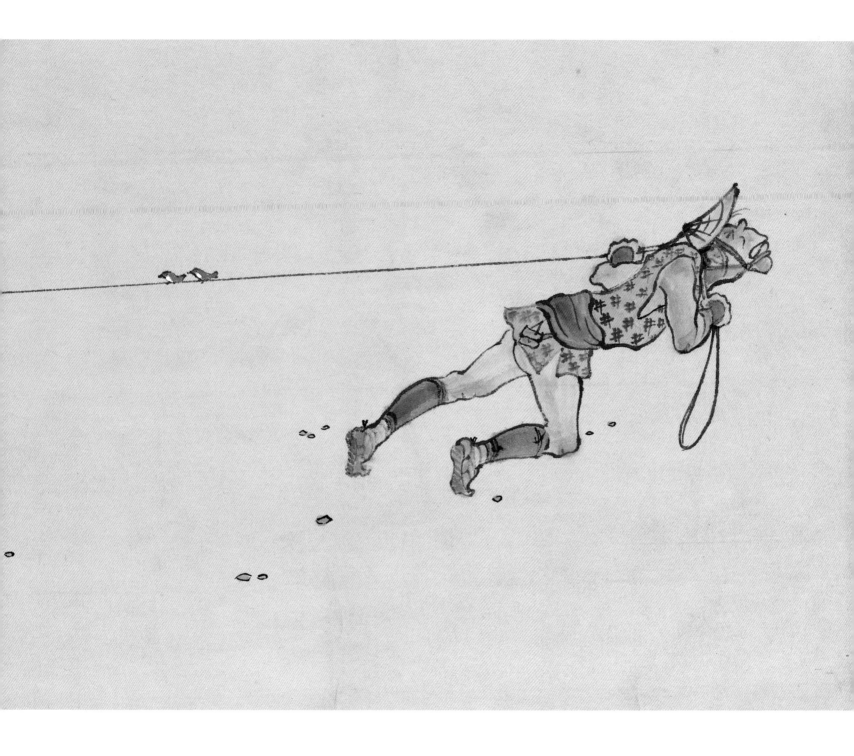

A man was pulling at it
trying to make it stand up.
"Oh please stop," cried Yohei,
"That poor horse needs a drink."

"That's too bad,"
snapped the man,
"I'm in a great hurry."

In desperation
Yohei produced his treasured rolls of silk.
"Wait, please,
I'll exchange you these rolls of silk
for your horse."

Of course the man eagerly made the swap
and hurried off
thinking how much money he would make
with the rolls of silk.

Yohei stroked the horse gently,
"Come on boy, come with me.
There is plenty of cool water
and sweet grass
not far down the road.
Come on now."

The horse struggled slowly
to the river bank.
Yohei felt content
as he watched his new friend
eat and drink.

Before long they were both refreshed.
On they went,
Yohei whistling a merry tune.

Yohei and his horse had not gone very far
when a man came running out
of a nearby house.
"Please, stop," he called to Yohei,
"You are just the man we need."
He then explained,

"My master has just received
an urgent summons from the Emperor
and must leave immediately,
but his horse is lame,
may we have yours
in exchange for this house and land?"

Yohei could only nod his acceptance of the offer.
"I must be dreaming,"
he mumbled as he stood
looking at his house and land.

"Let's away!"
ordered the Samurai
as he mounted the horse
and thundered off with his men in attendance.

Day after day
Yohei toiled from morning till night.
Soon his farm became
the most prosperous in the village.
Yohei and his new wife held a party
to celebrate their happiness and good fortune.

Everyone in the village was there
and late into the night
could be heard the sounds of singing and laughing.
Then Yohei told his story
which had begun with just
a piece of straw.

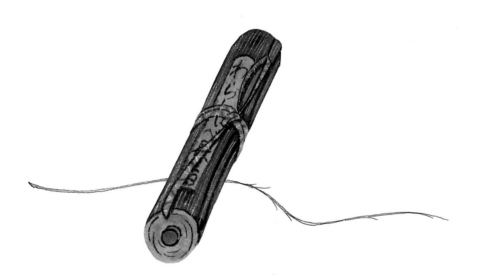